Joy and the Far Away Land

WRITTEN AND ILLUSTRATED BY
JOY SAXTON

This book is a true story about Joy's travels to Russia during the cold war with a performing arts troop called Peace Child when she was fourteen years old.

JOY AND THE FAR AWAY LAND

ISBN: 978-1-941515-84-6
Library of Congress Control Number: 2017951952

Published by LongTale Publishing
www.LongTalePublishing.com
6824 Long Drive Houston, Texas 77087

Design by Tamara Dever and Erin Stark for TLC Graphics, *www.TLCGraphics.com*
In-house Editor: Sharon Wilkerson

First Printing

Dear Child Reader,

Thank you for choosing my book to read.
I hope you really like it.

My name is Joy and this book is a true story, every single page.

It all happened to me many years ago when I was smaller.

I want you to know that I care deeply for all the children in our world. I spend each day of my life working to make this world a special place for you.

When you grow up, I want you to always remember to love all the people.

I believe in you,

Joy

Joy lived in a beautiful land where she loved to
paint rainbows and blue skies.
Her heart was filled with butterflies and joy.

Joy had Christmas parties, birthday parties,
and tea parties in her backyard!

When the moon came out,
she *danced* in the yard,
and every tree *sparkled* with fairy bugs.

Joy dreamed of going to far away lands
where there were magical temples and kingdoms.

She loved to sing and dance.
She auditioned for a traveling play and got the part,
but it was going to be performed in a far away land.

People began to tell her stories. They told her they
were fighting with the far away land, and the people
there were very bad. Joy became afraid
of the people in the far away land.

She decided to be *brave* and go to the far away land.
She packed her bags and said *goodbye* to her backyard.
She *promised* she would come back home soon.

She went on a *huge* plane that crossed *oceans* to get there.

Joy sang and danced
on a big stage.
The people in the far away land
loved her!

Joy made friends with a little boy
who was also in the play named Sergey.
Even though they did not speak the same
language they understood each other.

Sergey showed Joy his city.
In the town square, Joy saw old men
playing chess and kids playing ball.

Joy went to Sergey's home,
and they prepared a special dinner for her.
His family was very kind to her.
Sergey showed her all of his childhood photos.

Once, Sergey and Joy climbed very high up to the top of a hill.
They could see the far away land.

Joy was *sad* when the play came to an end,
and she had to go back home.
She said *goodbye* to the far away land and began to cry.
She promised she would *never forget* Sergey
and the far away land.

When she got home she was excited
to tell all of her friends about the far away land!

Back at home, she read in the news
that her country and the far away land were at war.

Joy became very sad because
her friends at home did not understand
why she loved the far away land.
She wanted the people in both lands
to love each other and to stop fighting.

Joy cried for the people in all the lands.

She thought a lot about Sergey
and the far away land
and hoped the fighting would end.

One day, Joy had an idea!
She decided when she grew up, she would tell all the children across the lands to not be afraid of one another.

When Joy was old enough, she traveled
to all the *different lands* to meet
the children and tell them her story.
She taught them to *love one another*.

The children she met *promised* Joy they would grow up and *protect* all the children of Earth.

Joy never stopped believing in the children!

About the Author

Joy Saxton began her career at 8 years old anchoring a local kids television show called *Kids TV Express* that won two national awards and aired for over ten years in Austin, Texas. Joy has worked passionately with children for over 25 years, teaching and developing programs that have made a difference in the lives of young children. She is the creator and director of the Joy Kids Studio where kids learn to write, direct, film and act in movies based in Houston. Joy wrote and illustrated *Joy and the Far Away Land* about her real life experience when she traveled to Russia before the end of the cold war with a traveling play called *Peace Child*. She lives with her husband, Bruce, and their two rescue dogs, Tinker Bell and Peter Pan!